THE TALE OF

BRACKET ISLAND

BEN MURRELL

First published in Great Britain in 2020
This paperback edition published 2020

Copyright © Ben Murrell 2015

Illustrations and Cover © Ben Murrell and Hannah Baker 2020
Edited by Rachel Mann

A CIP catalogue record for this book is
available from the British Library.

KDP ISBN: 9798633400335

sea orchids

[sea or-kids]

NOUN

1. Once land dwellers the tribe took to hiding in the shallow parts of the Valore Ocean during a war with the Goblins. Adapting to their surroundings they retreated to the depths of the Valore Ocean for survival.

2. A nickname given to the tribe named after the plant life that grows under water.

3. Have never been seen.

A LOST LEADER

Legends, fables and myths come from history. They all start from a single tragic moment that changes the lives of the people or creatures from the various kingdoms that exist. Some involve an evil queen filled with greed and hatred, others include a wish to change a life forever that never quite fulfils the true desire. Some are stories about gruesome beasts sworn to eat any living soul they encounter. Stories grow and evolve well beyond their original form, so that no truth remains in the tale that is passed on.

If you sailed further than the Seas Beyond the Shore, out in the middle of the Valore Ocean, you would find Bracket Island, which is not an easy place to navigate to.

The closest mainland, otherwise known as Nayalan, is linked via a bridge to the island. Nayalan is part of the Wye Quarter, one of four districts which are all made up of different colonies.

This particular island is not any regular stretch of land, as it once housed the sacred temple of Raxgore – King of the Sea Orchids. The first inhabitants to find the Wye Quarter were said to have been guided by Raxgore himself, who was an explorer and a land walker. No one knows the true story as to why he is now the king of the Sea Orchids. The townsfolk believe that he wanted to explore all the seas and the oceans and find what was hiding beneath the deep blue veil.

The myth is that Raxgore one day dived into the Valore Ocean and swam down as far as he could, until he could not hold his breath any longer. On his return he described what he had encountered: a tribe, and a sunken city hidden within the ocean of Valore. But how could Raxgore explore this city when he had only a limited amount of air?

He needed a sorcerer or a Mistress of the Herb—a woman who knew about potions and certain types of plants that were said to give the body special abilities.

There had been only a couple of ships that had brought people to this new land, so there weren't many whom he could ask for advice. A few of the new inhabitants spoke of a Jewel Nettle that produced pockets of air when the leaf became wet, allowing any swimmer to ingest the air bubbles and swim deeper. No one seemed to have seen this Jewel Nettle, but described it to Raxgore as a three-pronged leaf, long enough that it could wrap over and around his head and be tied around the back of the neck. It had mini spikes all over, but they were furry to touch, rather than prickly or stinging.

Raxgore collected all the information he could and searched the Wye Quarter for the nettle that resembled the one he needed.

We all know that when given only limited information, it's foolish to try to find something very powerful without anticipating consequences...and Raxgore ended up in this predicament.

He found what he thought was the Jewel Nettle on the rocky edge of Bracket Island. All his fellow shipmates, workmen and tribe that had sailed this far with him, supported him on this expedition.

Raxgore secured the nettle over his face and tied it round the back of his neck.

At first nothing happened, and the nettle sat loose on his face, almost dangling. *How is this going to help me breathe?* Raxgore thought.

Right before he was about to dive, the nettle tightened over his face. Was this meant to happen? Was this how the nettle worked? Raxgore had no idea.

He attempted to pull off the nettle, but it wouldn't budge. The others on the shore saw him struggling and ran over the bridge to the island to help. By the time they had reached Raxgore he had already dived into the ocean, sinking towards the city he thought he had discovered.

No one dared follow him down as they knew they weren't as strong a swimmer as Raxgore. How were they to save him? They couldn't. If he survived the ordeal, they thought, then he would have explored where he wanted to reach. And if he didn't then he had at least attempted it—a fitting end to an explorer's life.

The people who had travelled with Raxgore now had to carry on, set up a life and kingdom without a leader…and they did just that.

Stars passed, and a new colony was created on Nayalan. They searched further into the Wye Quarter and found that they weren't alone, that three other tribes also lived there, made up of all kinds of beasts and creatures, furry and not furry.

The Nayalans told them the tale of what had happened to Raxgore and the other tribes explained about the Sea Orchids who controlled the waves and the oceans. They also said that Raxgore *would* be alive but would remain so only if they as a tribe respected and honoured the Orchids in what they did, or the Orchids could destroy any coastal settlement in the greatest storm there had even been.

What could the Nayalans build to honour the Orchids? It explained why the seas had always been too rough to cross to Bracket Island since the day Raxgore disappeared. Maybe if they built something honouring Raxgore instead, who they hoped was now with the Sea

Orchids, it would calm the Valore Ocean so they could venture into it.

The other tribes each had their own monument to the Sea Orchids. The district of Ocktan had a tree they planted on the shore that grew Dalary Berries which they picked and threw into the ocean for the Sea Orchids. Ryisk had a stone fire-pit that stayed alight at all times, a beacon to the Sea Orchids to show them where the Wye Quarter was. Then there was the district of Fayoon, who did things slightly differently. At the start of every season they would hold a night of celebration for the Sea Orchids. The tribal dance and song of the Orchids would be played and this would send everyone in Fayoon into a trance, where they believed they would encounter the Sea Orchids. Though the creatures of Fayoon were hefty furballs and definitely not swimmers. They would sink quicker than they could swim. Maybe the sightings of this secret tribe were the Sea Orchids playing tricks on the mammoth creatures as a joke, no one really knew. However, the Fayoon tribal dance was their way of honouring the Sea Orchids and they stuck by it.

The Ocktonions suggested that the Nayalans needed something great as they had lost one of their own to the Valore Ocean. A monument so grand it depicted their true admiration for the Sea Orchids—a temple, and there was only one place it could be built – Bracket Island.

It took time, but with the help from the other districts the temple was constructed in the middle of the Valore Ocean, on a tiny piece of land. Four stone pillars were built around the edge of the small island as the start of the temple.

When they came to lay the floor they found a well hidden underneath the earth. No one on the Wye Quarter knew this well existed, or how it even got there. They contemplated venturing down into the well to see what was there, but then heard what could only be described as a faint, grumbling roar coming from the mouth of the well, they thought it wise to not find out. No roar was ever a welcoming sign and only ever seen as a warning. They thought wise to not let curiosity get the better of them.

The temple roof was made of terracotta tiles and sea coral with a peak in its centre and four corners that flicked up at the edges. It was perfect. The Nayalans could now honour the Sea Orchids and also their lost leader, Raxgore. Maybe one day he would return to see what a magnificent structure they had created.

The shrine was complete and the Valore Sea became peaceful once more. The Sea Orchids were pleased and approved of what the Nayalans had gifted them.

At the foot of the bridge that linked the mainland to Bracket Island, a plaque was made telling the story of the leader they lost to the sea.

The well was made into a permanent structure and they built it up out of the ground into a centrepiece for all to see. It was named 'The Well of Valore', and rumours to why the shrine was built and what was down the well soon started to travel far beyond the Wye Quarter, to the other side of the kingdom of Wilon.

These districts soon became known as the tribes who calmed the Sea Orchids. They were named the peacekeepers and the well became famous, with people believing it to have powers far greater than any sorcerer could conjure. The Nayalans had put themselves on the map…but at what cost?

JEALOUSY CAUSES CONSEQUENCES

Time, as it naturally does, passed and the shrine to the Sea Orchids on Bracket Island became more popular than the Nayalans could ever have imagined. Kings, queens, royal beasts and creatures from far and wide came to hear more of the Sea Orchids and what they did beneath the surface of the water.

The Wye Quarter was more populated than ever, and all because of the temple.

The travellers wanted to learn more about who and what the Sea Orchids were, other than the guardians of the sea. The Nayalans told their story of Raxgore and how he ventured to the bottom of the Valore Ocean to find out more about them.

However, the inhabitants of Ocktan, Ryisk and Fayoon could only speak about how they honoured the species they had never met, and it was the same for everyone in the Wye Quarter. They had no real facts about who the Sea Orchids were.

From this came gossip that turned into stories and finally manifested into legends. The centre point of all this was Bracket Island, the gateway to a land that was submerged far beneath the shore that lapped up against the jagged rocks to the temple.

The Well of Valore became a particular focal point and again the myths started to spread of how this well sucked in all the evil surrounding the Wye Quarter and that the Sea Orchids fed off bad thoughts. It was the mouth that fed the hunger and protected all who lived in the entire kingdom of Wilon. None dared to question the power of the well, or even venture down inside to see what truly existed at the bottom. Any that walked across the stone bridge to the island to take a look at the well stepped cautiously. People trod in fear that they would fall, trip or even be pulled into the well by the forces of the Sea Orchids.

The Sea Orchids, who none had encountered other than the Fayoons who claimed they had seen them during their celebrations, had become a tribe to be wary of…to be feared…to seek protection from.

Were the Nayalans to blame for this? They had built the temple in the first place, but under the guidance of the other tribes. Jealousy was growing within the Wye Quarter because of the popularity of the well and Bracket Island. The other tribes were not happy. A council meeting was called.

The leader from each of the tribes and their second in command were called to the Council upon the Wye chambers that were located in the centre of the Quarter where each of the lands joined.

The Nayalan leader, Linkx, was last into the board room and gently closed the doors behind him. The silence in the room was unnerving, it was as though he had done something wrong and was waiting to be punished for his actions. He took his seat swiftly while the rest of the room watched on. Linkx felt the judgement of every other tribe leader, making out like this was all *his* fault, but for what? Honouring the Sea Orchids like they were told to?

The Fayoon leader, Shifton, didn't fit comfortably around the square council table that was situated in the centre of the room. The oversized fur-laden beast perched herself on a custom-made throne to the left of where Linkx had entered. The sunken brown eyes, masked through the matted long fringe, were still piercing enough for him to feel uneasy—as anyone would with the Fayoon tribe. They were gigantic beasts that you stayed well out the way of. No one wanted to be trodden on by one of these. You wouldn't lose a toe, you'd lose a leg.

Linkx pulled his chair in and it scraped along the ground, flooding the air with a high-pitched squeal that was to no one's delight.

Ryule Jagon, leader of the Ocktans, spoke first. His mighty fist slammed down on the table to begin the meeting.

"The council are in session. What is said is to stay only within these chambers and no further enquiry is to continue outside of these walls, no matter how far you agree or disagree to the statements and arguments. No one will take further action against one another, without the agreement of all the council, and no person, beast or creature shall take the Wye Quarter Law into their own hands or paws to act out what one believes to be right. Do all present council leaders agree?"

"We do!" exclaimed every being seated around the council table.

"Good…now we can begin," Ryule added.

The council sat as grunts, coughs and fidgeting commenced for a few moments before anyone said anything. They knew why they had to hold this meeting, but it seemed no one wanted to be the first to speak.

"However much I do like spending time with all of you, and it is a treat every experience we have together, maybe we should start speaking about the topic in hand?" Linkx was never great at coming across as funny and once again his joke failed and only came across as rude and inconsiderate to the others around the table. Even his second in command, Eel, looked at him as if to say 'what are you doing?' There was a time and place for trying to be humorous and Linkx never got it right.

"Maybe you should start apologising for that temple your tribe built – that's the reason we are here in the first place!" Shifton seemed to have a grudge against Linkx and the Nayalans.

"Apologise? For what? I didn't personally build the temple on Bracket Island and plus, if I recall, it was the idea of all the tribes to build something that stood out, different to the Ocktans', Fayoons' and not forgetting the Ryiskys' offerings…"

Gelina, the leader of the Ryisk tribe, subtly shook her head at him for his comment. She respected Linkx and knew he meant no harm.

"But the meeting was called not because of *our* shrines …" Shifton said, "…it's THEIRS that is the problem!" she roared across the table to Linkx.

Shifton was not happy in the slightest; there was so much anger and hatred towards Linkx and the Nayalans. Linkx went to speak but Eel wisely grabbed his arm and suggested he didn't.

"Where has this come from? The Sea Orchids are not a tribe to be feared. They aren't evil, they don't destroy – all they ever wanted was not to be forgotten. I think you, Shifton, have mixed the hearsay with reality. Don't listen to the stories, that are only speculation, but remember back to when this land first began to why we celebrate the Sea Orchids as we do," Gelina said, attempting to calm the situation and ease tension.

"Yes, the temple and the well on Bracket Island are extremely popular, more so than our shines, but that doesn't mean ours are any less important," Ryule added.

"The only solution is to take it down! Keep the well, but the temple goes!" Shifton announced, with a hint of excitement in her voice.

"We can't take it down. It's still a shrine to the Orchids. They deserve that at least." Gelina said.

"But you know that's the only way to stop this. Take down the temple and the kingdom stops flocking to see the eyesore. Abandon Bracket Island and leave the well – the Sea Orchids need only that as their shrine from the Nayalans.

However much the table didn't want to agree, Shifton was right. For the moment this was the only solution in reducing the number of travellers and well-wishers to the Nayalan shrine. If the Sea Orchids didn't realise they were closing the shrine then there might not be any consequences.

"That temple, Bracket Island and the well will divide us all. It will become bigger than any of the tribe's shrines put together, just you see. Fayoons see more than simply what's in front of them. Ours will become the better shrine. Meeting over!"

Shifton threw back her chair and marched out of the room. The walls shook as she stomped out of the council chambers. Once a Fayoon was angry, it was never wise to cross them. The council let her go.

"Maybe we should think of a solution, each of us, and reschedule a meeting to discuss it further?" Gelina smiled gently.

"We can close off the Island for a while until we think of a way round this – we can say it's under maintenance," Linkx said, like a told off schoolboy. He knew it wasn't his fault but hated to cause any problems, especially over a shrine that was meant to be a good thing for the quarter and for the kingdom.

"I don't like the sound of that plan, but maybe for the moment we can monitor it, until we think of a better solution. It would reduce the numbers and also keep the Fayoons at bay and allow their jealousy to soften. I'm guessing it wasn't only me that picked up on that."

All the council and their seconds nodded at Ryule Jagon's statement.

"Let's hope the Sea Orchids either don't find out or disapprove of this temporary solution or we might just see if the legends are true. If we are the gateway for the sinful creatures that lie beneath the ocean, and if the well sucks in all the evil, it might just spit it back out as well."

CURIOSITY SHOULD BE KEPT A SECRET

The next day the sun glistened on the seafront in Nayalan. The Koo Koo birds had positioned themselves gracefully on the Valore temple to sing the morning tune that everyone had become accustomed too.

Pix and Eeray, who were brother and sister, squinted as the sun beamed in through the netted veil in front of the window.

"It burns…it burns!" Pix squawked as he rolled over on his bed, pretending that the sunlight was melting his skin.

"Don't worry Pix, the stinky-sock attack will save you," Eeray shouted as she rolled to the end of her bed.

"Huh?" Pix mumbled, having no clue to what was about to happen. Eeray swept the floor for any used, dirty, grimy socks from the days before and launched them at Pix as he lay in bed.

Inexperienced in stinky-sock attacks, Pix was unaware that in such a situation one should always close their mouth, tight. Eeray threw every sock she could find at Pix's head. He scrambled around to dodge them, but Eeray had become secretly good at aiming, with every sock hitting its target.

The last one she had she took focus. She pelted it at Pix, hitting the bullseye… his mouth.

Pix spluttered as the crusty sock touched his tongue.

"Ewww, Eeray that is gross!" he wailed.

Eeray fell about laughing – what a perfect start to her day. Not such a great one for Pix though.

With a sinister smile, Pix climbed up onto his bed. "You're in for it now, sis…"

Before he could attempt a comeback, Eeray spotted what he was about to do and barrel-rolled out of the room and dashed off.

"Hey! Come back, that's not fair!"

To Pix's surprise, Eeray was on fire today and the day hadn't even begun.

Both siblings, as early as it was, were now wide awake and ready for playtime. Other family members, however, didn't seem so keen on the idea.

"Will you two calm down! It's too early – the Koo Koo birds aren't even properly awake yet," Mist, Pix and Eeray's mother, informed them – but neither took any notice as they tried to catch each other out around the dining table.

Pix and Eeray could both be like animals at times –when they had something in their heads they would continue it until they either got too tired or injured themselves. This was one of those times, and Mist knew it was going to end in misery.

Eeray made a dash from the back end of the table, towards the main door outside. Pix was too far round the other side of the table to catch her, so attempted a diving take-down. As this played out, Linkx walked in through the main door, becoming a human cushion that both Pix and Eeray ploughed into.

"Woah!" Linkx yelled as he stumbled back through the door.

Both Pix and Eeray stopped, looking up at their father.

"Sorry!" they said in unison.

"I must admit, you two are growing stronger by the day – what have you been eating? Dalary Berries?" Linkx stood, chuckling at the thought that his children were one day going to be super-strong Nayalans.

"No, of course not, we know we can't eat them. They're for the Orchids," Eeray said light-heartedly, helping her brother to his feet.

"Well at least you remember. Just testing you," Linkx said, brushing past to finally get inside his own house.

"Last one to Bracket Island, turns into a Polup!" Pix shrieked at Eeray. The game had obviously not finished.

"WAIT!" Linkx bellowed, stopping both children almost immediately.

"What did we do?" Pix automatically went on the defence.

"For once, you didn't do anything. I need to tell you something, come back inside for a moment."

Pix and Eeray looked at each other, puzzled. Their father sounded serious, but not in a way that suggested they were in trouble or something tragic had happened, so what in Wilon could it be?

"Before you go racing off to the temple, I need to tell you something before the day becomes disappointing for you. Bracket Island, for the moment, has been closed off and is strictly out of bounds."

The jaws of the two children dropped, perfectly in sync.

"But why?" protested Eeray. "We love playing over on the island, it's sooooooo cool!"

"However coooooool it might be: one, you know the temple is sacred ground, so you shouldn't be playing up there anyway, and two, I can't go into the full details with you now as it's a matter for the Wye Quarter council – but one of the reasons is the bridge. It's becoming weaker by the day, so we need to fix the issue before it becomes a problem."

Both children looked at each other, knowing full well their father had gone into council mode. He was talking like he did in his meetings and they thought he must have forgotten he was talking to his own children.

"So, you can go play wherever you like but please stay away from Bracket Island."

"Ah that's not fair, it's the best place to play! Mum, did you know about this?" said Pix.

"Well yes, of course, your father tells me everything. He's my best friend, after all."

"Best friends?"

"No you aren't, you're Mum and Dad,"

"Just because we are your mum and dad doesn't mean we can't be best friends with each other, too. Aren't you brother and sister and also best friends?" Mist asked.

Pix and Eeray pulled a face at each other as if to say 'what?'. The two children clearly had never really thought about family like that.

"Go over to Bracket Island and see the precautions I have put in place. Also tell your friend, the Fayoon about the island being off limits, and then the three of you know *not* to go on there, no matter what. Got it?"

"Got it!" the children replied to their father.

"Now hurry, before I turn into an Orchid and bite off all your fingers and toes!" joked Linkx.

Pix and Eeray looked on in horror – obviously that rumour had reached the younger generation and no one had told them that that legend wasn't true. Once again, maybe Linkx had picked the wrong time to joke.

"I'm kidding, obviously. Can nobody round here tell when I'm trying to be funny?"

"Stick to swimming…" Mist patted his shoulder gently and pityingly, "…you aren't bad at that."

The day had started off interestingly but now what were they going to do? The temple was off limits, and the thing they loved to do best was to drop stones down the well and see how long it took before they hit the bottom. They knew they shouldn't, but like all children and young beasts, being intrigued about things would always come before caution. Most of the time the stone never hit the bottom and if you didn't hear anything you had to make up a story as to why – the terrifying tales were always the best.

Both of them solemnly made it to the start of the bridge that carried any visitors over the Valore Ocean and to Bracket Island. Linkx had put up a sign that blocked the path entirely so no one could miss it.

Bracket Island and the Valore Temple are currently out of bounds. The Council are addressing the issue and it shall remain closed until a later date.

Apologies to any explorers, travellers and well-wishers, please seek out the other shrines to the Sea Orchids located in the Wye Quarter.

Linkx
Council Leader of the Nayalans

Attached to the sign were tree vines marking off the area round the bridge and down the shoreline. It was clear to all that this island was closed and no matter who you were, nobody was to step foot onto Bracket Island.

"So where are we going to play now?" Eeray sounded disappointed.

"We could always sneak onto the island. No one would know, would they?" Pix suggested.

Then a voice rumbled from behind them.

"Don't you dare cross that barrier or you'll be in great trouble!"

It turned their stomach and made them quiver in shock. Someone had overheard them.

A MISCHIEVOUS PLAN

Pix and Eeray slowly turned round, expecting to see an overbearing Ocktan or, even worse, their own father. The one time they'd mentioned something slightly out of line, and of course they had been caught.

When they finally opened their eyes, they did not see what they imagined.

The voice did not come from high up, but from a creature much smaller than they'd been expecting.

"My impression gets you two every time," the creature giggled to himself.

"SMAAH!" Pix and Eeray shouted with delight, relieved that they weren't getting a telling off.

"I don't know how you do that, but it does get me every time... DON'T do it again!" Eeray joked as she couldn't really be that mean to Smaah.

Now, Smaah was best friends with Pix and Eeray and was a cub like they were children. He was a Fayoon – Shifton's son. Thankfully he didn't take any of the strict and sometimes stubborn qualities that his mother had. Smaah was a little different to the rest of the Fayoon tribe. He had shaggy fur that was always a little too long for his body. Most Fayoons would grow quite quickly in their cub years and then slow down when they were older. But poor Smaah hadn't really changed much in height since the day he was born.

Although that did have its advantages, as it meant he was quicker on his paws than any other Fayoon. This resulted in his muscles growing in a slightly different way and meant he could play with Pix and Eeray who were humans. Smaah could run, jump, climb, crawl – you name it, he could do it. For this he did get picked on by other Fayoon cubs, but Smaah didn't take any notice of them as he had the advantage. Also Pix and Eeray didn't care what he looked like, as he was their friend.

All three of them remembered the day they became friends – could have turned out very differently if Smaah had been a typical Fayoon.

When Pix and Eeray were a little younger they had been even more mischievous together. Not that that had changed much now they were older, but they were just better at not getting caught.

The children and cubs all mixed and played with each other, so no one in the Wye Quarter grew up thinking there was a divide between the tribes. Why would there need to be, when they were all in support of cherishing the Sea Orchid monuments?

Some of the Fayoon cubs had a den that they thought was the best den there ever was, and rivalled any den that anyone could ever make. They bragged about it so much they had even taken wood, vines and logs from some of the other children's dens from across the quarter. Their den was the best as it was made of all the other great dens.

The thing was that no other cub or child could stop them, as the Fayoons were always that bit taller and stronger than everyone else the same age.

Eeray especially, because she was older, had had enough of this. It was time to get their own back and retrieve the parts of their den they had lost. The battle of the dens was on.

Eeray had devised a plan to sneak into the Fayoon cubs den, and not only take back what was rightfully theirs but also leave another surprise. Frax, an annoying Fayoon, was the chief of the den and he didn't care if he ruined other dens, as long as his was the best.

"A rotting Solu fish!" Pix suggested. "If we hid it, they would never know what the smell was!" He did come up with some vile plans sometimes, but Eeray thought it a great idea as it was funny too.

Once they had searched the shoreline for a washed-up fish, they left it out in the sun until it started to smell, which wasn't very long at all, and the mission could begin.

Dusk was falling and Pix and Eeray watched Frax's den from a distance, perched up in a tree.

"Pewwwweee!" Pix exclaimed. "I can smell this through the sack. Can we go yet? I don't think I can hold this for much longer – it's making my head feel funny."

"Not yet. We have to wait for the Fayoons to leave the den or we'll get caught," Eeray instructed, and she had a valid point too. They couldn't leave the fish outside the entrance as it could be got rid of too easily.

They were in a safe spot for the moment, as Fayoons couldn't climb trees.

Finally, Frax and his gang left the den. Eeray guessed it was to go collect more wood, as all of them had left.

"Ok, now's our chance. We got to be quick and quiet. Do you understand?" Eeray said, as if she was on a real battlefield.

"Errrr, yeah?" Pix replied.

"DO YOU OR NOT?" Eeray emphasised in a loud whisper.

"Yes, yes. Go in, hide the fish, take what we can."

"Good. Let's go!"

So both Pix and Eeray climbed down the tree and scurried along the uneven ground to the den, attempting to stay out of sight.

They headed towards the back so they could peer in and see if the den was completely clear. It was.

"Ready?" Eeray mouthed and Pix responded with a nod. "Go!"

They both ran round the side of the oval den and headed inside.

They were in and safe, but they didn't have much time, as they didn't want to be caught pulling off the best prank ever.

"Where shall I hide it?" Pix said, slightly panicked.

"It doesn't matter as long as it's not on show – and make sure you take it out the sack too."

Each of them had their missions: Pix to hide the fish and Eeray to grab anything they knew was theirs, or at least anything they could improve their den with.

Within a few minutes Pix had concealed the rotting Solu fish in between two logs of wood that were the supports to the den. It was right in the corner where no Fayoon would see it. Eeray had grabbed a huge branch from the side wall, knowing she could drag it back along the ground. In doing so, she pulled down half the wall.

"Well, I think they'll now notice that someone has been in here."

Pix smiled. Perhaps the fact that half the wall was missing would distract the cubs from finding the fish.

If she had known this mission was going to be so easy, she would have brought back-up so they could take more stuff away.

"I think we should go, I don't like being here now," Pix warbled.

Eeray agreed.

They turned to leave … and standing in the entrance was a Fayoon. They had been caught.

Both children froze – but the Fayoon cub was pulling the same look of surprise. No one knew what to do.

"We didn't do anything!" Pix blurted out.

"Shut up, Pix," his sister slapped him on the arm.

"I didn't think you had…" replied the Fayoon. "I was here to do something."

"Huh?"

"Yeah, I came here to destroy the den but looks like you've already done it for me."

"Why would you want to destroy the den, isn't it yours?" Eeray asked.

The Fayoon laughed.

"No not mine. Frax picks on me so thought I would show him a trick or two. I can help you if you like, to get away and not get caught. I can carry that branch? It looks twice the size of you."

"Good plan, let's go!"

The two children and the Fayoon who they later found out was called Smaah, helped each other escape and became friends. If it wasn't for Smaah helping, they may not have made it out without being caught. They heard the cries from the Fayoon cubs when they had realised what had happened but the escapees were already too far away for them to be blamed.

From then on, a friendship had started. It may have been out of the strangest coincidences, but a good one nonetheless.

"We could always go play on the Tally Fruft Tree Stumps," Smaah suggested as something to do.

"Well if Bracket Island is off limits we don't have a choice, do we?" Pix said.

"There's only one thing for it…" Eeray shouted as she shuffled away. "…race you there!"

*

A few hours had passed, and playing on the tree stumps had become monotonous. Even the Koo Koo birds who watched on from the surrounding trees had succumbed to snoring – this had been an uneventful day.

Eeray was sat on the middle tree stump and swung her legs off, kicking her heels against the bark.

"I suppose … we could always try, maybe…" Eeray was eager to propose something but didn't dare say it, as she knew, deep down, they would get in trouble. "…going onto Bracket Island?"

There was silence. Smaah stopped gnawing on the stump furthest from Eeray and Pix sat up from lying on the ground.

"Aren't you two intrigued to know what's happening?"

"Not really. My mum said it was something to do with stopping all the visitors going to the well and to make our shrine look better," Smaah said, but he hadn't listened fully.

"So there's nothing wrong with it at all then?"

"Don't think so."

Eeray stood up on her stump, triumphantly.

"So who's with me to go to Bracket Island?"

LISTEN TO THE WARNINGS

The children knew the island better than anyone – which rocks you could stand on to see down into the Valore Ocean, and which boards on the walkway creaked when you stepped on them. There was nothing about the island they didn't know, other than the well itself.

"This is also our chance to take a look down the well – there'll be nobody around to stop us!" Eeray kept adding in reasons why their adventure was a good idea.

"You know we aren't allowed to, it's sacred," Pix reminded Eeray.

"We aren't destroying it or disrespecting it, we're only having a look down the well."

"I have always wondered what you can see down there…" Smaah said with a nervous smile.

They stood in front of the sign Linkx had made and contemplated the idea once again.

If they could make it across the bridge then they knew they wouldn't be seen. The island was so far out and no one from the shore would expect to see two children and a Fayoon on there anyway.

"We'll only do this once," Pix said, as a compromise.

"Well it depends what we find, doesn't it?" Eeray countered.

"Come on, quick, no one is here. Let's go." Smaah had lifted a vine so they could climb through, and both children followed.

The bridge rattled and trembled under their feet and paws as the three of them darted along it. All of them ducked lower as if this would stop them from being seen.

The bridge felt much longer than usual.

They headed for the rocks on the far side of the island and hid behind them briefly to catch their breath.

They ducked down to survey the area and to see if anyone had spotted them. They were in the clear.

"See … I told you … we could make it…" Eeray said catching any air she could.

"No you didn't … when did you …say that?" Pix gasped.

"Doesn't matter we made it and now we own the island, it's ours, mwahahaha!" Eeray evil-laughed.

"Yeah we own the island now!" Smaah threw a paw into the air. "Who wants to look into the well to nowhere?"

Of course, all of them did, but they had to do it carefully. If one of them were to fall in, who knows what would happen to them. But who was going to take the first look?

Eeray volunteered, as it had been her idea to put the group in danger.

The well was in the middle of the temple, directly below the peak in the roof. There was a barrier that circled the well, stopping anyone getting too close. Five wooden posts were secured into the slate floor and woven wine shoots were twisted together to create the wall.

The vines were so thick that it wasn't the case of pulling them apart and squeezing through—the three had to help each other over the first hurdle.

The vines squelched as they climbed onto them, and a sludge black liquid oozed out.

"Ewww that's gross, what is that?" Pix screeched.

"Don't let it touch your skin or it'll attach and you'll grow gills and turn into a Sea Orchid," Smaah replied in a serious tone.

"What? Really?" Pix jumped down off the vines and desperately shook his hands in case any of the liquid had touched him.

Smaah laughed in a husky roar.

"I'm only joking, look…" Smaah picked up some of the sludge and removed it from the vine. "It turns this colour because of the sea water. My dad was showing me cool things. Did you know you can mix tree vines with sea water and it turns into this? It's great when you want to scare people."

"You sure? You're covered in fur, I'm not."

"I'm sure."

Once the three had climbed over the first barrier they were trapped between it and the stone wall of the well. It seemed a little more menacing then they had expected up close—a bit too close for comfort.

"Can you hear that?" Eeray paused.

"Stop messing about Eeray, you aren't as convincing as Smaah. I'm not falling for your tricks." Pix urged Eeray to carry on climbing.

Smaah and Pix braced themselves against the cold harsh surface wall of the well so Eeray could climb up and peer down into the well.

Hands were placed on heads and feet almost in mouths. The two hiked up Eeray until she was at the edge, feet away from the entrance to the well.

"I can almost see down, just a little higher!" Eeray called.

"We're trying!" Smaah replied, struggling to keep Eeray where she was.

"This hurts. Eeray you're too heavy!" Pix cried, scraping his face against the stone.

"If I can reach a little further I can pull myself up." Eeray stretched out her arm to try and grab the furthest part of the well. If only her fingers would grow a little, the tiniest bit, and then she could grab the stone with her whole hand, but it seemed that wasn't to be.

"I heard it again. Did you hear it that time? A rumble, a murmur, I felt it in my skin that time…" Before Eeray could continue or even get an answer from the two holding her up, they all indeed heard something. It was a Ryiskian gliding towards them over the bridge.

"Excuse me! Excuuuuuuuse me!" the voice shouted.

"Quick – get down, Eeray, you've been seen," Smaah said, pulling at her leg.

"But I'm so close!"

"It's too late, we've got to go."

The three of them erratically helped down Eeray in the panic of being caught. There was the odd bump and scratch that no doubt all of them would feel later, but right now the pain was subdued by the fear.

"Quick this way!" Pix indicated that they should hide in the area they had originally climbed over at the back of the well.

They scrambled over the vine barrier, only to find themselves face to face with Gelina.

"Well aren't you three rebels in the making?"

"We…"

"Didn't…

"It was her idea…"

Smaah, Pix and Eeray all spoke at once, rambling over each other, defending themselves and accusing one another, as that's what all young children and cubs did when they were caught doing something they shouldn't have been.

"Whoa, relax. I'm not going to get you in trouble. We are all a little mischievous from time to time, even me in my younger days…"

"Really?" Eeray blurted out. She wouldn't have expected a council leader to say that.

Gelina glanced her a look as if to say 'are you interrupting me?' Eeray was in no position to be talking back just yet.

"…the thing you have to master is not getting caught." Gelina winked at the three sorry faces in front of her. "Now, you know you are not allowed on here, it's out of bounds to all for safety reasons. You two especially should understand that, as it was your father who appointed the ban."

"Sorry," both Pix and Eeray said, solemnly.

"I won't say anything to Linkx or Shifton if you promise me you won't do it again. We don't want to cause any more issues than we may have already done by closing off Bracket Island in the first place. I know you must be intrigued by the well, as we all are, but doesn't mean you should disrespect it by climbing all over it. Maybe some things are best left unexplored. Do we have a deal?"

The three instantly nodded. There was no way that either of them wanted anyone else finding out about what they had done, especially Linkx or Shifton.

"Right, on you go and re-fix the barrier you seemed to have squashed somehow. You three are a strong little number aren't you?"

Each of them gave a smirk, taking the hint of a compliment, and left the island over the bridge they first entered on.

"I heard something too, when I was pushed against the well. Maybe it was the wind inside, but I definitely heard something," Smaah whispered to Eeray.

"Gelina did say some things are best left unexplored…but the well isn't one of them. We have to find out what's down there."

They had been defeated in their attempts but were going to take on Gelina's advice. Not the bit about doing it again, but the part about getting caught. They needed a plan this time, one that meant success.

Pix wasn't too keen on playing over on Bracket Island again. He hated being told off, even when he knew he was in the wrong. Eeray convinced him that this time they wouldn't get caught at all and they could have a look in the well and then that would be it.

"Don't you want to know what's down there? We would be the only people in the whole of the Wye Quarter who had stared into the darkness of the Well at Valore. We would be legends to everyone."

Pix did like the sound of that, and so did Smaah. He wouldn't get picked on for being small anymore, and all the other cubs would want to know what he'd seen. The time had to be right, though – they couldn't do it at night amongst the shadows as they were only young and had to be home by a curfew. This didn't leave many options, other than to repeat what they had done last time, and that hadn't worked out well.

So they waited. It would be at short notice, but they all agreed that when it was time, they were going to execute their plan.

*

Bracket Island continued to stay off limits and abandoned for a while. Many explorers and visitors had been turned away and unable to take in the wonder of the Island.

The three liked having their own little secret and told no one else, as they didn't want rumours spreading.

Days rolled by, which nearly turned into seasons, when something started to change in the Wye Quarter.

Winds had picked up and dark storm clouds were approaching from the west. This was a rare sign to see, so the council met to discuss what was happening.

"Meeting has commenced in order to discuss the approaching storm and the provisions we may have to take if it strikes," Ryule stated at the table.

"I assume we have angered the Sea Orchids. It's their way of punishing us. Bracket Island has been left for too long and they have noticed," Gelina said, worried.

"Gelina is right. I need to open up the temple and the well. Surely now we can put this behind us, Shifton. We have deterred folk for long enough. Depending how angry the Sea Orchids are, the storm could be a violent one. We all remember the stories of past and how savage the sea can be," Linkx pleaded with Shifton.

"Do as you wish with the island. I care not for your temple any longer, when we are building something greater of our own. Our shrine has been dismantled and we are in the process of creating something magnificent. So thank you, Linkx and the council, for your patience in this, but the Fayoon tribe are happy with the progress we have made."

Every heart in the room stopped for a second, if not slightly longer.

"You've done what?" Ryule boomed deeply.

"You know you can't take down a shrine—what were you thinking?" Gelina panicked which was a rare sight to see.

"Is it any wonder a storm is heading our way! This is your fault, you've angered them just so you can make your shrine better than the Nayalans'. It's not a competition, it's about honouring the Sea Orchids. The Wye Quarter do things collectively." Linkx's words were wise, and for once the whole room agreed with him, even Shifton. Deep down she knew she had made a big mistake by dismantling the shrine, although she would never admit to it.

"It was never going to be for long. A re-build into something greater. The foundations are still in place…" Shifton started to backtrack on her earlier statement.

"The Sea Orchids would never care how grand something was, it is merely the gesture, the sentiment that makes it special," Gelina added. "It seems you didn't think about the consequences of your actions."

"Then we shall re-build it now, if you think it'll affect us all so much. But it'll be only another storm that'll pass by…"

"Whatever it is, it looks like it has already started." Linkx stared out of the window to the mist growing in the distance. They all knew that meant rain and lots of it.

"Get your team to build as much of the shrine back to what it was as quickly as possible. We may be lucky—this could be a regular storm and not anything summoned by the Sea Orchids," said Ryule.

The council members left immediately with Shifton first out the door. Her own hurriedness told the council she knew she had made the wrong choice. Her own jealousy, not even the tribes, had potentially put the whole Quarter in jeopardy. She could only hope this all was nothing but a passing cloud.

*

Smaah, Pix and Eeray were on the outskirts of the Nightsglare Wood when they noticed the treetops starting to sway heavily. The dark clouds loomed overhead as a few spots of rain fell onto Pix's skin.

"We best head home, it looks like it could be one of those storms. I didn't like the last one," Pix walked ahead a little faster.

"That's because you are younger and scared of everything, even your own reflection," Eeray said, as Smaah giggled huskily.

"No I'm not!" Pix protested. "But if everyone else is going to be inside then so am I."

"Wait a minute, what did you just say?" Eeray asked wide eyed.

"So am I?"

"No the bit before, about everyone going inside."

"Yeah don't you remember the last storm we had, it was so heavy with rain that no one was allowed outside…"

"That's it!" Eeray interrupted so excitedly she was bouncing off the ground. "We go now, to the well. If we go before the rain starts properly then we won't get wet but everyone else will already be inside. Come on, run!"

The other two looked at Eeray. She had a point. This was the moment they had been waiting for. The rain was the distraction they needed, so they could take a proper look into the well.

They kept out of sight by using the trees and darkness surrounding them as the thick grey clouds blocked out most of the sunlight.

The rain had begun to come down heavier as they reached the bridge. The Valore Ocean also looked a little different, the waves were crashing up against the rocks and the bridge, as though the sea was trying to drag down the temple into its violent waters.

The bridge was soaked which made it difficult to cross, more so for Smaah who had no grip on his paws and was sliding all over the place.

They made it to the temple as the clouds and the winds combined to lash the Wye Quarter with all it had. The rain was so heavy they couldn't see the shoreline anymore, their distraction was better than they had hoped.

"Let's take a look and get back before people start to wonder where we are," Eeray said, making her way around to the back where they had entered before.

The ocean was rough and they were covered with spray every time the waves hit the side of the rocks. The quicker they got this done, the drier they would stay.

"Come on, hurry. My fur is soaked already, do you know how heavy it can get when it's wet? ... Very!" Smaah complained.

"Right, well this time you look first then, so you can stay dry behind the vine barrier when you help us up." Eeray made a fair point, and this meant Smaah would then be first out of everyone to take a proper look.

It was easier for Smaah to climb up as he was stronger than Eeray and Pix put together. If he had been a typical Fayoon he would've stood no chance, but with such power in his legs, he was up in only two pushes.

Smaah stood on top of the well as the chaos continued around him. He edged towards the hole in the well to peer over.

"What can you see?" Pix shouted up to him.

"Nothing yet, I haven't looked!"

"Hurry up then, I want to see," Eeray also shouted impatiently.

Smaah shuffled forward slowly, trying to keep his balance with the winds howling around the temple. Maybe the storm wasn't a good distraction after all.

He stretched his neck forward as his eyes followed the depth of the well down to as far as he could see.

"SMAAH! LOOK OUT!" Eeray shrieked, as a huge wave came smashing over the side of the rocks, ploughing straight into the fur-laden creature.

Pix ran round the well to find where Smaah had landed, but no Smaah was to be found.

"Smaah? SMAAH! He's gone! He's gone down into the well!"

WHAT LURKS IN THE DARKNESS

The storm raged on, becoming angrier the longer Pix and Eeray spent on Bracket Island.

"We have to go," shouted Pix over the raucous sound of the ocean.

"We can't leave Smaah, we have to get him out!"

"I know but look, the bridge…"

Pix pointed. The bridge was starting to crack and twist from the bombardment of waves. "We'll go get help, quick before it's too late for us."

They had no choice, they had to leave the island and come back for Smaah later. There was so much going on around them, there wasn't time to think.

Pix led the dash back to the mainland and dragged Eeray behind him.

The bridge had snaked at the end and the last few boards had come away from the shore, so the children had to jump to make it back on to solid ground.

They hit the ground hard and rolled over. When they got to their feet again they looked back and watched the remainder of the bridge collapse and be washed away into the ocean.

"NO!" Eeray cried as she imagined Smaah down the well on his own and now with no way of getting back to save him.

"Quick Eeray, we have to go," Pix grabbed his reluctant sister and they ran in the pouring rain back to home.

They slammed open the door into the arms of a worried Linkx and Mist. Both Pix and Eeray were in such shock that they couldn't find the words to say to explain what had happened. The tears rolled down both their faces as the sky thundered and roared to its own spectacle it was displaying outside.

Linkx and Mist asked the children why they were so upset. Neither Pix or Eeray said a word. There wasn't even a shake of the head or a stutter of words.

Both had almost frozen. Their best friend had fallen into the most sacred place in the Quarter. How could they tell their parents this, especially when they had been told not once but twice to stay away from Bracket Island?

The thunder clapped once more which shook the pots dangling from a rail in the kitchen. Pix jumped at the noise.

Linkx and Mist grabbed the two children for a cuddle and assumed it was because of the storm that they were so upset.

Pix and Eeray never worried about a bit of heavy rain. In any other circumstances they would be outside trying to play in it, against all warnings from their parents. However, it seemed that both children had subconsciously decided to not to tell the truth and keep the incident with Smaah a secret.

Time would tell if the lie was a wise choice or not.

The next morning the storm had subsided, but the clouds stayed close, as if they were ready for act two at any moment.

The Wye Quarter had taken a hit, especially Nayalan. Linkx went to inspect the temple and what he saw wasn't good.

The bridge that connected the mainland to Bracket Island was completely gone, as if it had never existed in the first place, and part of the roof of the temple had been ripped off.

Others started to gather to see what had happened as the news had spread.

"How did all the other shrines bear up?" Linkx asked as he was joined by Gelina.

"Fine I believe. Shifton and the Fayoons managed to get some of the old one rebuilt before the storm hit fully. Maybe this wasn't to do with the Sea Orchids after all. I'm sorry to see what this has done to Bracket Island though. We'll get this fixed so don't worry."

The whispers circulated amongst the hundreds that were now standing on the shore to Bracket Island:

"Was this the work of the Sea Orchids?"

"I hear it was the Fayoons who caused this?"

"I told you those Sea Orchids weren't to be messed with."

No one knew the facts and Linkx had to say something. But before he could get the chance, a triumphant roar bellowed out of the well, shaking its surroundings.

"It's the island, we have awoken the beast in the well!" someone shouted. It happened again and this time the people and creatures screamed.

"It's all our fault, we should have never angered the sea dwellers!" another voice cried.

The roar happened a third time and sent people into a panic. The crowd deserted the shoreline and headed back to their homes.

"What are we to do, Linkx?" Gelina said as she waited for advice.

"I don't know, I really don't know."

The days passed but the noise from the well continued and Linkx declared Bracket Island to be an area of the

Wye Quarter that no one would ever venture to again. The Valore Ocean had taken it as hostage and maybe if they left it alone then the Sea Orchids would see it as a happy compromise to the lack of respect the Fayoons had shown. Bracket Island was fast becoming a place where evil lurked. Where the shadows would look like creatures that roamed the island looking for trespassers. For now, the awoken beast was trapped inside the well, warning off any who dare approach it.

Pix and Eeray knew the real story, they knew it was Smaah calling for help, but what could they do? If they told anyone, they would get into trouble because they had been on the island when they shouldn't and by now if they said something, no one would believe them. Especially if they said he was down the Valore Well. No one was brave enough to take on that rescue mission even if they did believe it to be true.

The Wye Quarter was being searched by the Fayoons for Smaah, as it seemed a lot of the tribe had gone missing during the storm. Whether they lost their bearings or got trapped in a sinking mud pit, search teams were in full force, but not one person or creature stepped close to Bracket Island—that wasn't theirs to check any more.

"We have to go and save Smaah, it's been two days now and he must be hungry, let alone scared!" Eeray said to her brother.

"I know, but how can we? We can't even get to the island anymore."

"Smaah is our friend, we'll find any way we can to get to that island, swim if we have to. We know the island isn't full of evil, and that noise is Smaah calling for us."

Eeray was right and Pix agreed.

"Wait, doesn't Dad have a small boat tied up down on the Far North Bay? We could use that to get to the island," suggested Pix.

"Sometimes Pix, you are a genius."

The children headed straight down to the bay and found the small two-person boat with oars attached to either side. They took along some rope they had found in a junk pile next to where they lived. It was Linkx's 'just in case pile' that had never come into use until now.

They both got into the boat and made their way over to the island.

Now that the majority of this side of Nayalan had become abandoned, due to the supposedly evil goings-on at Bracket Island, they had a safe passage with no one stopping them. How could they even if they wanted to? There was no bridge or anyone brave enough to approach, apart from the two children to save their friend Smaah.

Pix and Eeray tied the boat up to a rock and climbed up to the well. The vine barrier had been destroyed and washed away, so it left the well open and easier to access. They had also found that part of the well had fallen down, so they used this to climb up to the top.

Now was their chance to look down inside. It was an endless tunnel of nothingness, apart from a slight blue ripple that was so small it may have been their eyes playing tricks on them.

"Tie the rope around the post of the temple and we'll use that to lower ourselves down." Eeray directed to Pix. "Don't worry, Smaah we're coming to rescue you!" she shouted into the well, but all she heard was her own words echo as they spiralled down into eternity.

With the knot tied they threw the remainder of the rope into the well and hoped that it would reach the bottom.

"I'll go first and then you follow me, alright?" said Eeray. "Just remember to hold on tight."

"Got it, sis."

All the excitement of looking into the well and finding out what was in it was now completely gone. They had to focus on rescuing Smaah, as it was their own fault that he was there in the first place.

They lowered themselves down further and further as the light around them began to vanish, eaten up by the darkness that seemed to get thicker as they descended.

"My hands hurt from the rope, Eeray."

"It can't be much further now, just hold on. And whatever you do, don't let go."

"My hands are slipping, I can't help it!"

Eeray decided to move quicker on the rope, if Pix was going to let go maybe she could get to the bottom in time to help him, if not catch him somehow.

But Pix slipped on the wall of the well and let go of the rope. He plummeted towards Eeray, knocking her off the rope.

They fell, though not for long, and landed in a heap of soft sludge. It broke their fall but with little light they had no idea what it was they had landed in.

"Urrrggghh, it's cold and squishy, what is it?" Pix said as he held up his hands to watch the goo slime its way down.

"I don't know, but at least it was a soft landing. Now we need to find Smaah and get him out of here."

Although dark it seemed there was a tunnel to their right that did have torch lights dotted along the path. Did someone live here? Or had Smaah had the clever idea to set this up?

"Smaah!" they both called. "It's us, we're here to rescue you, Smaah!" But there was still no response.

"Maybe he climbed out and already went home? Maybe we missed him?" Pix said.

"How? We struggled to get down here with a rope, let alone without one. No, he must be here."

They wiped off most of the gloop that had saved them from injury. Although soft it didn't smell great.

They both stood at the entrance to the secret tunnel.

"I guess we explore this way?" Eeray suggested.

A gush of wind started to build behind them which followed with a blasting roar.

Maybe they had been wrong about the well, maybe it was full of evil, as the roar hadn't sounded like Smaah at all.

"Let's get out of here!" Eeray pulled Pix towards to rope and they started to climb.

Just as they got to the point where the well exit met the ceiling, Eeray came face to face with a huge eyeball. All it took was one blink for them both to scream at the top of their lungs.

This was the monster living inside the well. This is what the Sea Orchids had kept a secret all this time and now it had its dinner.

LOST BUT NEVER FORGOTTEN

Again they fell and landed in the sludge. As quick as they could they scurried back, terrified at the monster with the huge eyes, the sharp teeth, the shaggy fur that was a little too long for its body...

Eeray noticed something about the humongous beast.

"Smaah? Is that you?"

"About time you two showed up. How long have I been down here? I'm so bored," Smaah replied, as friendly as ever.

It sounded like Smaah but a little deeper and he looked like Smaah but a little bigger.

"Wow you've grown, haven't you?" Pix looked up to see how far Smaah reached.

"Yeah I finally grew and now I'll fit in with all the other Fayoons. Frax won't be saying anything now to me. And all it took was for me to fall down a well."

Not only had Smaah grown, he was super-sized. In the tunnel he couldn't tell but Pix and Eeray could see it, he was taller than any other Fayoon there ever was. But how did he grow so quick? He hadn't been down here for seasons or even stars, why was he so big?

Smaah explained what had happened since he fell.

"I got stuck in the sludge and I couldn't move, not with all my fur anyway. I thought water was bad until I got covered in that stuff. Once I wiped all of it from my eyes there were loads of strange creatures in this cavern. I was scared at first but then they helped me and were really nice. One introduced himself as Raxgore…"

"Wait, Raxgore? He's a Nayalan, the first one to the Wye Quarter. He's here?!" Eeray had remembered the story Linkx had told her.

"Well yes and no—he's a Sea Orchid now, one of the leaders actually, and they all helped me out and took me down that tunnel to get me clean. Anyway since that happened, I started to grow. The Sea Orchids couldn't believe it either. They think it must have been a reaction from the sludge, which comes from the secret reservoir that is sacred to the Sea Orchids. So many explorers supposedly go searching for it, it's called…err…I always forget the name but it's another well, another entrance down here. Ah that's it, the Well of Treau. It's believed to grant people's desires, not that I believe in that…"

"But you're tall, so it must have worked," Pix pointed out.

"No this is what all Fayoons do, they grow big and strong!"

Pix and Eeray looked at each and were not convinced.

"But I got to meet the Sea Orchids and all the stories aren't true about them. They even made up some of the stories for a joke to see what the Wye Quarter would do. But now you're here, let's go, I want to go tell everyone about what I saw. We are going to be legends. You were right, Eeray, after all."

"But how…" she said disappointedly. "How are you going to get out?"

"Through the well again, I'll just climb up the rope with you two."

"But you won't fit, you've grown too big to fit back up!"

Smaah hadn't realised that when you grow taller, you can't do the things you used to do before, like hide up trees or sneak around or fit down wells.

"Then how am I going to get out of here?" Smaah asked.

"I don't know, but we'll work out a way," Eeray said firmly.

The two children asked what the other entrance to the secret underground cavern was like and whether he could escape that way. Smaah told them that he hadn't fully explored as it was quite far away, but the Sea Orchids had said it was hidden deep inside a creek. They explained how at the moment Smaah was too short to climb out and the path that spiralled down from the top of the creek was too thin for his paws to fit on to follow it out.

The Sea Orchids were looking after him and Smaah was happy to stay for the moment until they worked out a plan.

So, they had to make do with the predicament. There is always something good that comes out of a bad situation and Pix and Eeray were not going to make it worse for Smaah, even if they did blame themselves.

Every day the two children visited Smaah down inside the well to keep Smaah company and to play like they used up to on the land. This became more fun as this was *their* little secret and they didn't want anyone else to know about it. It was extra special when you were the first to explore somewhere. Smaah showed them around the areas he had been to and what he had found. The children actually started to prefer being with Smaah in their secret hideaway—the best den that any cub or child could ask for.

The longer they took to devise a plan, however, the taller Smaah grew. It wasn't going to be long until he didn't fit in the tunnel at all, and would need to make his way to the Treau Well for a bigger area to live in.

This made Smaah sad. Would he ever be able to leave and go back to playing like he once did in Nayalan with his best friends?

Pix and Eeray knew that no matter what happened they would still visit him every day, as that's what best friends did. Eeray would keep her promise to him and think of every way possible for him to be able to leave.

Stars had now passed and the children had also started to grow taller. They would never reach the size of Smaah, no Nayalan ever would, let alone a Fayoon. Although that was a good thing, as by staying small they could climb onto Smaah's back and he could carry his friends any place he wished in the underground tunnels.

Pix and Eeray even got to meet some of the Sea Orchids too, the only people ever to truly see them up close. They had to promise not to say anything to anyone. They had become experts now at keeping secrets so adding one more was no problem.

One day when they were playing around the entrance to the Treau Well, Raxgore approached with something he wanted to ask Smaah.

"Just the Fayoon I needed to speak to."

"Not that you know any others," Smaah cheekily replied.

"No this is quite true. I need to ask a favour of you, an important one."

"Ah, what is it?" Pix was intrigued.

"Don't interrupt, you," Eeray slapped her brother on the arm. "Sorry about him."

"It's quite alright," Raxgore chuckled. "I too was once like you and everything intrigued me, which is why I found myself here. Anyway, I digress. Smaah, as you know this reservoir here is very sacred to us and you have witnessed the power of the water. More and more explorers are trying to find this place and not for their own use but of others. Kings, Queens, evil sorcerers, lots of people with bad intentions want to use this water and not for the greater good. There is only so much the Sea Orchids can do from the sea, on land we are vulnerable and lack the defences we master within the waters. I need your help to guard the well, ward off anyone who tries to enter and test them if you must to see if they are worthy of it. It will be a challenge at times but your roar alone I know is very powerful…"

Smaah let out a tremendous growl that made both Pix and Eeray jump.

"…exactly! Will you do this for us, help us protect the one thing we have? The one thing that helped you become the great Fayoon you are today?"

Smaah thought about it for a second.

"But that means I'll never be able to go home, doesn't it? Go back to playing in the Quarter. Doing what we used to."

"Smaah, we can play here. We've seen you every day since you fell down here and that's never going to change. If you went back now, the Fayoons wouldn't recognise you. *We* know you, they don't…" Eeray attempted to ease Smaah's mind but came out in the wrong way.

"I never said you couldn't go home, we just don't know how to get you out. But one day we will, you have my promise—as well as Eeray's—on that," Raxgore added.

"Hang on…" Pix suddenly became excited. "This is a brilliant idea. This could be the best game there ever was. You get to scare away anybody that tries to come down here, Smaah, into *your* home. You get to play tricks on them and fool them all the time. This is the best game EVER!"

"Oh yeah…" Smaah had a think. "I do like to scare people, it always makes me laugh. And I could try all the pranks I wanted to do on Frax and his cub gang."

"This is the biggest game you'll ever play, Smaah, and everyone in the kingdom of Wilon will know of you and not to attempt to trick the Fayoon who guards the well," Raxgore smiled.

"And with my two assistants to help me, Pix and Eeray. Would you two like to join me?"

They both nodded furiously with wonderment at all the tricks they could play.

"Then Smaah, for those who dare cross your path and enter the Smaah Creek, I announce you Keeper of the Well of Treau."

If you enjoyed this adventure and want to explore the world of Wilon further, then try:

THE BOOKCASE
VEIL OF SHADOWS
and
RISE OF A LEGEND

All part of The Ink Dwellers Trilogy

For more publications and information by
Ben Murrell follow…

facebook.com/murrellben

Printed in Great Britain
by Amazon

13358707R00048